KINGMAKER

CONNOR WHITELEY

No part of this book may be reproduced in any form or by any electronic or mechanical means. Including information storage, and retrieval systems, without written permission from the author except for the use of brief quotations in a book review.

This book is NOT legal, professional, medical, financial or any type of official advice.

Any questions about the book, rights licensing, or to contact the author, please email connorwhiteley@connorwhiteley.net

Copyright © 2023 CONNOR WHITELEY

All rights reserved.

DEDICATION

Thank you to all my readers without you I couldn't do what I love.

CHAPTER 1

Assassin Ava Oakley really did enjoy planets that were like old Earth before the coming of the emperor, the superhuman Angels and all the other things that followed to make the glorious Great Human Empire.

Ava stood behind a large thick oak tree that was easily three times as thick as she was tall, and she was hardly a short woman, standing at just over two metres tall. She still loved it whenever she got mistaken for a man, that was classic.

And it really helped her in her line of work.

Ava pressed her gloved hands against the rough tree bark that sent cold chills up her arms and into her armoured body. She loved the coldness, especially in times like this when she needed to be extra focused and alert for any possible signs of danger.

The sound of animals groaning, shouting and whistling to each other sounded like a deafening thunderstorm in the middle of the forest where Ava was. The smell of pine, cinnamon and peanuts filled the air from nearby trees and Ava really hoped that the smell would mask her scent even more. Even if it didn't, it still had the amazing benefit of leaving a wonderfully strange taste of pecan pie on her tongue.

Being an Assassin was great fun, and Ava couldn't be happier travelling the galaxy killing the enemies of the Emperor and dealing with all possible threats, no matter how small or so-called grand.

Sometimes the other assassins in the various Assassin Guilds would ask her what her favourite kill was, but that was the biggest difference between her and the other Assassins.

She actually didn't like the killing.

Ava was an assassin to save lives, protect the Empire and keep people safe. And if there was a way to do all that and not kill everyone, she would do that way. Not kill.

But after decades of killing, protecting and slaughtering, the reality of that strange ideal really wasn't living up to what Ava had wanted when she first entered the Guild as a little child.

Ava wanted to keep humanity and the Empire safe, no matter what. And she was going to do that regardless of the cost.

The sound of people rustling through the forest made Ava smile and she focused through the dense oak forest and towards her prey.

About twenty metres ahead of her was a massive clearing in the forest where there were five brutish looking women standing around metal crates. That's what Ava had wanted, but she was really waiting for their boss to arrive.

As an assassin, Ava was never sent out from the safety (prison) of her Assassin Guild unless there was killing to be done, and a big enough danger to the Empire that the Emperor and the Empire High Council had decided that an assassin was needed.

Ava still found it funny how everyone in the entire Human Empire believed that assassins were cold, murderous demons that were happily spilt their throats as they slept safely in their nice warm beds. But that wasn't true.

Sure Ava was an extremely gifted assassin and she truly believed she could kill anyone and anything, but she didn't kill innocent people. That was not only a law amongst Assassins but a personal principle too.

So when the Emperor himself had contacted her (Ava still couldn't believe that had actually happened!) and told her about a Traitor operative smuggling ancient nuclear weapons onto the planet she was currently on. Ava wasn't going to turn down this mission.

Ava had read about these awful weapons in history books, and whilst there were far worse weapons that could annihilate planets in a second now available, these ancient nuclear weapons had to be stopped.

The sound of engines roaring and slowing down made Ava carefully look up at the sky as she saw a small pod-like shuttle start to descend and land in the clearing.

Ava started to glide from tree to tree as she got closer to the clearing.

The brutish looking woman stood at attention and now Ava was so close, she could see these women were wearing former-Empire Army issue armour. These women used to serve the Emperor, and now they fought against him.

They were definitely going to die for that abominable act.

The only problem was Ava didn't know where the nuclear bombs were. The information she had been given proposed the nukes were little metal balls about the size of these things called *footballs* from Old Earth.

Ava didn't know where they could be.

Ava pulled out her little metal pistol and double checked that all the high-explosive rounds were in place, and that everything was working.

Granted, high explosive rounds didn't sound like something she wanted to use around nukes, but Ava just wanted to have a little fun.

And try not to die in the process.

The pod-like shuttle started to drop a staircase down and out came a very tall elegant looking woman.

Ava instantly recognised her from pic-feeds, criminal records and even her Army Service Record where she had been gifted one of the Empire's most prestigious awards.

Adeline Elliot was going to die today.

"Weapons?" Adeline asked like she was a Commander of the army.

The brutish women crossed their arms and the metal crates started to float off the ground and into the pod-like shuttle.

Ava let out a breath she didn't know she was holding, at least she knew there was no chance of hitting the nukes with any of her own bullets.

Ava watched as the Brutish women got closer to Adeline. They didn't seem happy but Adeline was only smiling.

Ava aimed her pistol at Adeline's head.

"You will be paid in full," Adeline said coldly.

"Listen here," one of the Brutish women said, "we hear ya wanted for treachery against the Throne. Emperor offering five million credits for ya capture,"

Adeline just shook her head.

Ava didn't need to hear any more of this. She really didn't need any extra factors that would complicate her kill.

She fired.

Her bullet screamed through the air.

Smashing into Adeline's head.

Vaporising her body.

The Brutish women exploded.

The shockwave ripping them apart.

Ava carefully went over to the killing ground and smiled at all the amazing, utterly wonderful pieces of charred flesh that littered the ground. It smelt amazing.

Then Ava simply looked at the pod-like shuttle. She might have been an assassin, but Ava could thankfully fly and at least she didn't need to arrange transport for the nukes now. At least she could simply fly it back to Empire Forces.

Ava's head buzzed and hissed as the assassin microchip inside her head (that she barely remembered most of the time) buzzed.

"Activate," Ava said.

"Kingmaker!" the chip vibrated into her mind.

Ava's blood ran cold.

She had only heard of these types of operations before, and assassins were so rarely used to assassinate Planetary rulers and replace them, that something dire had to be going on.

In the past three hundred years alone, there had only been one Kingmaker operation and that had ended horrifically, and billions of people had died.

So whatever was going on, Ava was concerned.

She felt like the fate of billions rested on her shoulders.

And her blade.

And that's what excited Ava.

Far more than she wanted to admit.

CHAPTER 2

Head of House Rosia Finn Scott sat in his favourite metal chair on his balcony that overlooked the entire capital of Decimus Prime, the jewel of the solar system and the Capital of the sector.

Finn flat out loved staring out in the morning watching the utterly amazing sun rise in the east, shining so bright that it turned the tall metal spires of nearby buildings, apartments and offices into glimmering diamonds that lit up everything so perfectly.

Finn really loved his planet. It was so amazing, and critical to the Empire. The Empire he really, really loved.

Ever since he was a little boy aged five earth years old, Finn had dreamed of leading this planet, system and sector into a golden age where everyone could benefit from the Empire instead of the rich Houses.

Granted he used to be one of the rich Houses,

until his father had assassinated by the King. So now the House of Rosia (as far as Finn was concerned) was nothing more than a dying jewel that ruled over the Western part of the capital and he tried his best to protect everyone.

The warm sun gently warmed Finn's fine black suit that was tailor made and shipped from Earth as a thank you present from the High Council for his work on getting the planetary government to conscript more soldiers for the Eternal War.

Finn still wasn't too sure if that had been the right decision, but he wanted to protect everyone in the Empire. So if the Empire needed more soldiers to fight, then Finn was going to give them to the Empire.

Finn looked down at the little black metal table next to him, and he picked up a tiny mug of rich black coffee. Finn loved the black stuff, especially when it burned like battery acid. It left his throat feeling alive, awake and ready to take on the day.

Which during these dark times Finn felt like he was all he could do as his planet descended into chaos around him.

Finn had no idea where it all started but about one Earth-Year ago, the current King had started to talk about seceding from the Empire. Everyone knew that was a death sentence, but the people seemed to love the idea.

And even the other five Noble Houses seemed to love the idea more and more.

Finn didn't understand that, three of those Noble Houses had actually made their money, power and influence off the back of massive Empire Crusades against different aliens. It made no sense for them to want to secede.

But Finn supposed after the first few assassinations of pro-Empire supporters, everyone had gone in line to various extents. Even Finn's own mother had been executed for so-called drug dealing, which was a flat out lie and everyone knew it.

Finn really hated the current King Jamie Pastor.

He had to die.

But as Finn had found out in the past few weeks of being Ruler of the House of Rosia, he really wasn't a fighting man. He was a politician and the people in the West of the capital loved him. But he was never going to fight anyone.

Finn just hoped (and really, really hope some more) that the Emperor would think this was a serious threat and somehow deal with it.

Even that was a scary idea. Some planets that wanted to secede were just burned to the ground, and billions of people died. Other planets were simply allowed to secede until a military attack force was sent to reclaim the planet. Again more deaths. And extremely rarely a new Ruler was installed.

Finn was never going to admit this in public, but he really wanted the latter to be an option. Finn wanted to be King and he honestly believed he would transform the system for the better of everyone. The people, the system and the Empire.

"Dad!" a young woman shouted.

Finn looked into his massive office and saw his young (she was fifty years old to his two hundred years old) daughter Fiona was quickly walking into the office holding a black dataslate.

"What sweetheart?" Finn asked.

"King Pastor is announcing the Secession in two days," she said.

Finn instantly put his coffee down.

"That means…" Finn said, "if the Empire get word of this, we would all be annihilated in two days,"

Fiona frowned. "He's an idiot. He's already said he's sent word to Earth and he's already got all Navy to form a brocade around the system to stop any attack ships from coming in,"

Finn just shook his head. He wanted more time to find a political solution. Finn had wanted to convince the King the error of his ways and maybe there was a chance that Pro- and Anti-Empire people could live in peace.

That clearly wasn't going to happen.

"There's more," Fiona said.

Of course there was. Finn just shook his head.

"Pastor has ordered the military to execute all known Pro-Empire people, not including the House of Rosia,"

"But who knows how long that will last," Finn said.

"Exactly," Fiona said. "Any word of those still loyal to the Emperor?"

Finn actually laughed at that. As much as he loved Fiona, he was still amazed that she thought loyalty was fixed and couldn't be changed. Clearly she wasn't really watching what was going on. The entire sector of space had been loyal once, now it was all turning against the Emperor.

"All our friends," Finn said, "have turned against us. The House of Rosia is the only loyal element left in power on Demicus Prime,"

"What are our options?" Fiona asked.

Finn smiled. "We have two options. Or things we need to do. In case there are loyal forces trying to make it into the system, we need to create an opening for them in the blockade,"

Fiona nodded. Finn knew she would like the sound of that, and she probably had an ex-boyfriend she could ask for help.

Then Finn realised what he was asking her to do, and he knew she would sadly do it. he was asking her to break laws, protocols and the Will of the King.

A death sentence for sure.

Finn tried to force it all out of his mind.

"And we need to try to stall the political conversation for as long as possible," Finn said.

"You want to call a meeting?" Fiona asked.

Finn nodded. "Thankfully the King has already called a meeting, but your mission is far more dangerous,"

Fiona slowly smiled. "Come on dad. Mum died for the cause. Grandaddy and grand-mummy died for the cause. Why not me?"

Finn frowned. He couldn't lose anyone in this fight against the King turning traitor. He didn't want her to die. She was his favourite daughter, he damn well loved her.

Finn hated even thinking about his wife that the King had murdered. Most days he felt bad enough without having to reexperience all that agony.

"Dad," Fiona said slowly, "why didn't you send me away with my brothers?"

Finn just looked away. He hated that he hadn't sent her away with the only other two children he had. He wanted too so badly, Finn's wife had demanded it, but he… just wanted to have someone he loved close.

Now just the idea of that selfish act would probably cause the death of his daughter… Finn felt like he was truly dead inside.

"I love you," Finn said, "and I knew if anyone could help me. It would be you. My smart, clever, beautiful girl,"

Fiona smiled and kissed Finn on the head one last time.

"I love you daddy," Fiona whispered. "For the Emperor,"

"For the Emperor," Finn said as he watched his little girl walk away for the last time as she went to do something that was suicidal but hopefully so critical to their freedom.

> Finn couldn't let her do it.
> But she had to do it.
> And Finn just felt numb.
> Finn just felt like an absolute failure.

CHAPTER 3

After six Earth-months of travelling, Ava finally stood on the small circular bridge of the Emperor's Shadow, a small spy-class cruiser, and she was furious.

Normally Ava had absolutely no problems travelling through the coldness of space for months at a time, it didn't bother her in the slightest. Especially when she got to regroup with her amazing teammates, but she didn't like planets threatening to secede from the Empire.

It was just stupid!

Ava had tried to understand all the utter nonsense before. Some planets said that the Empire was too oppressive, others said the Empire was too weak, and even more idiots just say they wanted to rule their planets exactly how they wanted to.

All of it was as stupid as each other.

But Ava would definitely be lying if she moaned about how amazing space travel was, it wasn't often she got to take out a spy-class ship and she loved it when it happened. Because there were so many amazing things packed into these ships like advance weapons, medical supplies and plenty of other things mere mortals could only dream of.

Ava stared out through the massive floor-to-ceiling window and onto the massive blockade in front of her. There were hundreds if not thousands of blade-like cruisers, destroyers and Emperor-Class Annihilators just waiting, sitting and preparing themselves.

Ava really did admire the balls of these people. Not only had they declared Secession from an Empire that needed and loved and respected them, but they were willing to go to war with them.

That was just suicidal.

There was absolutely no other way to put it.

Ava was grateful that the Emperor's Shadow was cloaked with some of the best technology in the entire Empire. But she didn't want to be here any longer than needed.

It also didn't help her that they had been given another mission. Not only did Ava and her teammates need to get onto Decimus Prime and start their Kingmaker mission, but they needed to scan and transmit data on the fighting force in preparation for a full military assault.

Ava didn't want to know why the High Council believed it was needed, but Ava had her job and she only focused on that. And it could actually make the Kingmaker mission easier, with everything distracted by an assault and invasion, it might be easier to move undetected around the planet.

Ava doubted it, but she damn well hoped.

The smelt of burnt oil, greasy hair and bad breath filled the bridge as the pentagonal doors swished open and in came Ava's two teammates.

Ava forced herself to look away from the blockade and she smiled at her two most favourite people in the entire Empire.

The short little woman with her long blond hair, dangerously thin body and six grenades attached to her waist was a junior Assassin called Bella Lee. Ava normally didn't like juniors, because they were simply too inexperienced, annoying and unbearable. But for some reason (and Ava really didn't know how) Bella had managed to earn herself the smallest amount of Ava's respect.

"Master," a short man, by the name of Ronnie Duncan, said.

Ava loved how Ronnie always looked so intelligent with his bionic eyes, dirty white lab coat and the holographic computer that was built into his arm.

He was probably one of the most amazing people Ava had ever met, and she would never ever say it (or want her people to think she was a soft assassin) but she did love his arms. She was always impressed with how he had an arm for every occasion. An arm with a built-in computer, a machine gun or maybe something else entirely.

She was really glad to have him here.

Ava loved them both, and knowing she was doing a Kingmaker mission was bad enough, but with these two close by she felt like she could actually achieve this impossible feat.

"Ronnie," Ava said nodding.

"Ava we have a transmission from The Grand Master Assassin," Bella said, calmly.

Ava admired her for remaining calm. Just hearing that they had a transmission from one of the most dangerous assassins in the Empire was enough to make her stomach tense. This was a massive deal, and even though Ava was getting transmissions from people who she had admired for decades more and more recently, she was still getting used to all this.

"What did the transmission say?" Ava asked.

Bella smiled. "It's live. Should I patch it through?"

Ava almost jumped at the chance to actually speak to the Assassin Grand Master of her Guild, but she made sure she looked cold, controlled and calculating in front of Bella.

Ava nodded.

"Patching through now," Bella said.

A moment later, a large blue hologram formed in the middle of the bridge with a tall man cloaked in a long cloak so Ava couldn't even see his face, or if it was a he at all.

"Assassin," the Assassin Grand Master said, his voice booming.

"Grand Master, it is an honour," Ava said, trying to keep her emotions in check.

"Our mission is clear. You are to reach the planet, kill the king and guide a Loyal member to their throne. We must control the Decimus system and the sector,"

Ava nodded. "Of course my Lord. But forgive me, I know there is something grander for you to be calling me,"

Ava could have sworn she heard the hologram laugh a little.

"It is little wonder the Emperor chose you personally. I must warn you, you have a secondary objective that is almost as imperative as the first,"

Ava felt her stomach tense. It was bad enough talking to someone she idolised, and now he was saying there was something almost as dangerous as this particular system and sector seceding.

"Assassin," the Grand Master said, "intelligence reports confirm there are five Hydra Legion operatives on the planet,"

Ava almost coughed and stopped breathing as the news smashed into her. Hydra Legion operatives weren't only superhuman soldiers designed by the Emperor himself that turned traitor, but they were infiltration specialists.

Ava had fought them multiple times, and each time it was ridiculous. Even now she was flat out amazed at how these massive superhumans could infiltrate the most protected of places completely unseen.

Each time she fought them it was like fighting smoke in the dark.

"I will kill them as the Emperor Wills it," Ava said.

"Good," the Grand Master said. "Transmit the data as soon as you can. The battle fleet needs it. The Emperor Protects,"

"The Emperor Protects," Ava, Bella and Ronnie said as they cut the link.

Ava just focused on the massive blockade. It was going to be next to impossible to get past all of them without being noticed, especially once they started transmitting all the data back to Empire forces. But it was a risk that Ava had to take.

She had to take it to protect herself, her team and her Empire.

"Data collected Master," Ronnie said. "Transmission of all available data can begin when you command it,"

Ava nodded. "Thank you. How long do we have until they detect us? And how long until they lock onto our position?"

Ronnie frowned. Ava couldn't blame him, these spy-class ships were amazing and normally none of this would be an issue, but it was because they were transmitting so much data so quickly that this was becoming an issue.

"Thirty seconds until detection. Another ten for locking on," Ronnie said.

Ava looked at Bella. "How long until we reach Decimus Prime?"

"Travelling at top speed. Two Earth-Hours,"

Ava hissed. She hated those numbers, but it was the best they had.

"Deactivate all weaponry, limit life support and turn off all non-critical systems. Direct power to the transmitting. The sooner we transmit the data, the sooner we can lose our foes," Ava said.

"Confirmed," Bella said as she completed the instructions.

Ava smiled at Ronnie who had activated his holographic computer and prepared to start the transmission.

"Ready?" Ava asked.

"Ready," they both went.

"Launch!" Ava shouted.

The ship shot forward.

The transmission started.

The enemy ships moved.

Ava was located.

Missiles were launched.

CHAPTER 4

Fiona Scott knew she was going to die in a few minutes, but she had to help her wonderful planet, family and most of all, her dad.

Even as she wore a long elegant white cloak that completely covered her face and body into the system's naval headquarters, she wasn't sure why she was doing this. All she needed to do was ask an ex-boyfriend who was still loyal to the Emperor to give a Naval Commander some new orders.

On the way over here, Fiona had carefully predicted that the most important fleet to move was the very first fleet any Empire forces would hit, and as she walked into the Headquarters more and more, she could see that something had grabbed that fleet's attention.

So it might be even easier to get them to move.

The headquarters was filled with tons of rows and rows and rows of tall, proud men and women that hunched over their computers relaying, giving and demanding new orders from the headquarters to the ships themselves.

But the saddest thing about all of this was how amazing each of these soldiers had been back before all of this.

Fiona used to work in the Navy, she was a very good strategist, and worked with almost everyone in this headquarters, and now they moved against the Emperor.

The brilliant man they had all sworn to love, protect and serve. They had all betrayed their oaths and they were all going to pay for that.

"Enemy Spy-class Cruiser detected!" a man shouted.

Fiona recognised that amazing sexy voice so clearly. Captain Nathan Julius was such a good, sexy man back in the day and Fiona really hoped he would be useful one last time.

But just in case, Fiona gently pressed under her cloak and thankfully she was still wearing the explosive vest that had been attached to her life signs and chest. If these traitors killed her, then there was no way Fiona was letting them live and fight to destroy the Empire she loved.

None of these people would be hurting anyone she loved.

"Alpha Fleet attacking," Nathan said.

Fiona kept walking towards him and she saw him hunched over his little holographic computer watching the action unfold.

Fiona subtly went over to him.

"I need your help my love," Fiona said quietly.

Nathan stopped. He didn't dare look round.

"I can't help you anymore. The Emperor is dead on this planet. Please run," Nathan said.

Fiona loved hearing his smooth sexy voice that still sounded so caring for her. Even though it was him who ended things and said that the military was more important than she would ever be.

That gave her an idea.

"You broke our relationships by saying the Emperor was more important," Fiona said.

Nathan huffed.

"Please tell me you didn't ruin our relationship for a lie,"

Nathan huffed again and started typing on his computer.

"Spy-class cruiser detected missile blasts!" Nathan shouted.

"The Emperor hasn't given up on us. The Emperor loves us. He has sent people to help," Fiona said.

Nathan laughed a little. "You and your family always were idealist. This is the real world Fi. I have to follow my orders,"

Fiona looked around. Thankfully no one had seen her yet, but she didn't know how much longer that could last.

"Forget orders. This is our system, our Empire, our everything at stake. Your mother, sisters and brothers are still alive. They will die if our Secession happens,"

Fiona felt the cold metal barrel of a gun press against her head.

"You called them," Fiona said quietly.

Nathan nodded.

Fiona slowly turned around to see a very familiar face. Supreme General Colson had a face savaged by war and he was one of the Empire's greatest war heroes, it almost broke Fiona's heart to see him working with these traitors.

"Relax," he said, "your father will join you soon enough,"

Fiona just shook her head. "All of you! The Emperor made us. He protected us. He loved us. You are all nothing. You are all worse than the superhuman traitors we all fought together two decades ago,"

Colson smiled. "You're wrong,"

Fiona smiled. She always loved how deluded these traitors were.

Colson's face flashed, flickered and for a second Fiona could have sworn she saw someone else. A superhuman of sorts with a massive twisted, scarred face that looked smashed and repaired so many times, it didn't look like a true face anymore.

"Colson died a long time ago little lady," Colson said quietly.

Fiona smiled. She had heard of superhuman traitors but she never thought she'll see it.

Fiona looked at Nathan. She just wanted to see his handsome face one last time.

"Please Nathan," Fiona said, "stop them. The Alpha Fleet must be moved,"

Nathan didn't even react to her. He simply kept doing his work, typing away on his computer like she wasn't even here.

Colson gripped Fiona by the throat. "If I wasn't busy, I would so have fun with you first. Maybe a little flaying of the flesh, a nibble of the skin, and many, many more delights,"

"Done!" Nathan shouted.

Nathan shot up.

Whipping out his service pistol.

He fired into his computer.

Destroying it.

Colson pushed Fiona away.

And shot Nathan.

Colson looked at the position of Alpha Fleet.

"Bastard!" Colson shouted. "He ordered the fleet to move. He ordered them to deactivate communications. They fucking think loyalists are in here!"

Fiona smiled. She had done her job. There was just one more thing to do.

Colson rushed over. Picking Fiona up by the throat.

"I'm going to fucking have my way with you girl!" Colson shouted.

Fiona smiled. "No you aren't,"

Fiona threw her head back as hard as she could.

Snapping her neck.

And as she felt the last of her life signals disappear. She heard the explosive vest activate.

Ripping the rest of her body and the traitors apart.

CHAPTER 5

As Ava sat in the front row of the massive rings of pure strong marble that created the seats of the Amphitheater she was in as she stared down at the golden throne and immense black stone table down below, she was starting to get very interested in what was happening.

This definitely wasn't one of the best amphitheatres she had been in during her assassin life, the ceiling alone was dull and was far from ornate. It was hardly the grand symbol of power that most Planetary Governors tried to make it, considering this was apparently the room where all the decisions of power were made.

Ava had only been planet-side six hours, just long enough to get Bella and Ronnie set up in a secret location, but not long enough to have a good understanding of everything that was happening.

But there was clearly something afoot.

From all the Empire data Ava had received by

the Assassin Grand Master, there shouldn't have been any major resistance left to this stupid idea. But when she arrived Ava had watched the Army try to put out the System's Naval headquarters.

It had been bombed.

And it was strange enough when the fleet that was attacking her, her ship and her team had suddenly stopped.

Ava wasn't willing to put her life on it, but she was fairly sure the Empire still had some powerful friends here.

The crowd of other people talked, muttered and groaned all around her as it turned out everyone wanted to see their deranged and suicidal King make the formal announcement to his people.

Ava wanted to burn these people for their betrayal and hatred towards the Emperor. The brilliant man who had transformed this lifeless system into the thriving one that they had clearly taken for granted.

And all their smells of smoke, sickness and drugs made Ava want to gag. These people smelt so disgusting that she was surprised these people could do much of anything.

Ava was even surprised the King allowed such wide ranging people to use these drugs, but he probably didn't care, and the King probably only used these drugs to make his people more submissive and work hard.

Ava had to stop him.

That was the easy bit though, and Ava hated it. The killing was always easy, the hard part was making sure a worthy candidate took over.

That really worried Ava.

"Master," Ronnie said through Ava's earpiece.

Ava was really glad she had left Bella and Ronnie back in their secret location, and she was here alone. Babysitting them was the last thing she wanted to do.

But just in the extremely rare event these drugged up people could actually hear something coming from the earpiece, Ava subtly adjusted the volume with the holographic bracelet she always wore.

And it contained an emergency teleporter just in case she needed a quick escape.

She just hoped she would never need it.

"The Rulers of The Noble Houses are in coming," Ronnie said.

A door must have opened under the amphitheatre as Ava watched men and women dressed in the fine coloured robes of their houses. Everyone wore their formal robes, headwear and even a massive ring with the seal of their house.

Ava had no doubt they were going to have to sign the Royal Decree Seceding from the Empire.

That was the moment Ava wanted to watch. She needed to see if anyone hesitated and if anyone had the support of the (drugged up) people, that could be the person to become King, or Queen.

Slowly each member of the Noble Houses looked at each other, smiled and sat down carefully.

Every moment was done so elegantly and carefully like one wrong step could kill them.

It probably would.

Ava focused her attention on each of them and noticed that each one was trying a little too hard to look in favour of these decisions. So much so that Ava was actually starting to doubt how much power each of these Houses really had.

"King is approaching," Bella said.

Ava smiled as she watched a very muscular, well-armoured man in golden armour stride in and sit at the head of the black stone table.

The King was rather attractive considering how much of a traitor he was, and Ava was really looking forward to killing him. There was something so satisfying about killing attractive people, it made her feel... powerful.

Then Ava noticed there was an empty seat next to the King and judging by the strange looks the other House Rulers and the King were giving the empty seat. It was clearly someone important.

Or someone they needed to deal with.

"New arrival incoming. Armed. Holographic pistol at the ready. Guards don't know about it Master," Ronnie said.

Ava smiled even more. Whoever this missing person was, they were clearly interesting and definitely had a death wish, but maybe a loyal death wish.

That would be interesting.

The entire room filled with the sound of hissing a

set of doors presumably opened and a very tall...

Wow!

Ava just stared at the utterly gorgeous sexy man that walked in. Ava was just shocked by his strong muscles that were barely kept hidden behind his tight bulletproof t-shirt, his strong jawline and the most amazing blue eyes Ava had ever seen.

This guy was sheer perfection.

Even the way he marched towards the King was stunning, elegant and just damn well sexy.

And even the way he held his gun was sexy-

"Gun Master!" Ronnie shouted in her ear.

Ava blinked a couple of times and focused on the sexy man with the gun. He was pointing it straight at the king, but Ava wasn't worried, there was a thousand different ways this could all go.

But everyone was tense.

After a few seconds, the two men laughed. The King shook the sexy man's hand and they both sat down.

Yet Ava couldn't help but feel like everyone else didn't know what that was all about. All the other House Rulers seemed extremely tense now and like they were about to make the biggest mistake of their little pathetic lives.

That was because they were. And if they dared signed something supporting the Secession.

Then Ava was going to have a lot of fun killing them.

And that really, really excited Ava.

Maybe not as much as the sexy man, but very, very close.

CHAPTER 6

Finn seriously tried not to stare at the holographic gun that was just sitting there in front of him on the massive black stone table, he hated the King and the other House Rulers.

Finn just wanted to kill them all.

As soon as he had heard about the explosion at the Naval Headquarters he just knew that his daughter had been killed beforehand. He knew how clever his daughter was and now these traitorous bastards had taken her from him.

Maybe Finn should have tried harder himself, he should have stopped her, he should have killed the King so long ago!

The disgusting, overpowering smell of the King's earthy aftershave was just too much. It was like the idiot King was actually daring to show off his wealth in front of the House Rulers he had made broke.

Finn just hated him.

Before the idiot King started speaking, Finn

looked up at all the blank drugged up faces of the people who decided to come and see this so-called historic event. Finn wasn't impressed with any of them, he knew for a fact that none of his people from the Western Capital would come.

He was grateful for them.

But there was a woman staring at him. Finn had to admit she was strange and sort of out of place here. She wasn't drugged up, looking happy nor sad. She was just staring.

Or not.

Maybe she was studying everything, everyone and maybe even him.

Finn actually wouldn't mind being studied by her because she was absolutely beautiful with her smooth skin, long brown hair that looked so soft and velvety and even her body from here looked perfect. Finn was really starting to feel drawn to this woman, but the only problem was Finn knew she was probably an ally of the King.

So he would have to kill her eventually.

Finn always hated to kill, but this was for the sake of the Empire and all of humankind. He couldn't allow some emotions to cloud his judgements, especially after he basically allowed his sweet beautiful daughter to sacrifice herself.

The entire chamber fell silent when the King clicked his fingers.

"Thank you Lord Scott," King Pastor said slowly. "It is an honour to have all of you here today,"

Finn just wanted to shoot him right now.

The King took out a large sheet of real paper that had been handwritten and Finn's stomach instantly tensed. He knew this was the Secession Document.

"Sign this," the King said coldly, "and say your peace,"

The King started to pass the document round and every single other House Ruler smiled as they signed it.

"With this signature, I damn the Empire to kill itself," the Ruler of the House of Darkness said.

"I hope the Empire choke on their corruption," the Ruler of the House of Waterlilies said.

Then the document got passed to Finn and everyone stared at him with a smile.

It was at that moment that Finn just knew everyone knew he wasn't going to sign it. Everyone wanted him dead and he knew he had no more friends left to save him.

For some reason (and Finn really didn't know why), he just looked up at that stunning beautiful woman who was just smiling at him.

She was so beautiful.

Finn grabbed the document and ripped it up.

No one gasped. No one moaned. No one did anything.

"I'm glad I got everyone to sign the real document earlier," King Pastor said.

All the other House Rulers laughed.

"I also got everyone to sign legal documents that

explained exactly what was to happen when I died. Be it by your hand, the Empire's hand, by anyone's hand. There is a direct line of succession so whatever you plan, it is useless,"

Finn just shook his head. He had been so stupid. He should have been smarter and not revealed his true intentions so soon.

"And the House of Rosia is no more," King Pastor said. "As we speak the military is going door-to-door grabbing every man, woman and child in the Western Capital. Everyone who believed in you will be sent off to Mind Camps,"

Finn coughed. Shit!

Sure he had believed the King had gone mad in recent years but now this was all confirmed. Finn and his daughter and sons had spoken about the traitor superhumans and their mind camps that could and would make even the most loyal man turn against the Emperor.

Now Finn knew for sure the King was in league with the Traitors.

That idea terrified him. Especially considering how much manpower, weapons and ships the Decimus System and wider sector made for the Empire. Finn couldn't allow all that power to fall into enemy hands.

The King picked up Finn's holographic gun and pressed it against Finn's head.

"Good bye Former-Lord Finn Scott," the King said.

A shot went off.
The King's head exploded.
The beautiful woman jumped on the table.
Grabbing Finn.

CHAPTER 7

Ava activated her emergency teleporter.

Everything disappeared in a cloud of blue smoke.

Seconds later Ava really smiled to herself as she reappeared in the cold blackness of the square apartment where she had left Bella and Ronnie to set up as their own little private base of operations.

Ava still couldn't believe how utterly amazing the kill had felt. She wasn't sure if she was going to take the shot, but as much as she hated to admit it (she wouldn't if anyone asked) she wasn't going to let a hot sexy man die when he was loyal to the Emperor.

And Ava had to admit, he had some balls. Ava was sure she could have said a very long list of military commanders that never ever would have ripped up an illegal document in front of traitors.

But this man had.

And that was hot.

The flat smelt damp, mouldy and unloved. Which was one of the reasons why Ava had picked it, there were so many different escape routes, but not many ways into the apartment block so they were all as safe as they could be deep inside enemy territory.

The very low sound of holograms vibrating, humming and swirling filled the air as the lights slowly turned on and Ava stared at the dark grey concrete walls of the flat, Ronnie and Bella, who was pointing a gun at the sexy man.

"Security threats?" Bella asked.

Ava just looked at him and he was beautiful, sexy and Ava so badly just wanted to have her way with him right at this moment, but she was a cold calculating Assassin first. Human second.

Ava watched the man and his perfect mouth try to form words, but he was too scared, frightened and concerned to do anything. Ava just frowned, a man that got scared at a little gun was hardly that attractive.

"No," Ava said. "The King's dead?"

Ronnie activated his holographic computer in his arm and presumably monitored all the official and unofficial chat about what had just happened.

"Confirmed Master. King is dead. Everyone is on high alert for Finn Scott and a strange woman. Orders are to kill on site," Ronnie said.

Ava liked that. She loved having the enemy scared, nervous and very likely to make stupid mistakes.

"Who are you people?" the sexy man asked.

Then it twigged and Ava realised that he was

Finn Scott. Ava wasn't sure if this was what she imagined a Lord and House Ruler to look like, the ones she had normally killed were fat, ugly and abusive. Finn didn't look anything like that.

But in her experience looks could be very, very deceiving, she had to be careful.

"I am Master Assassin Ava of the Emperor's Assassin Guild of the Dagger. And you are a very stupid man,"

Finn laughed. "I just... wanted to serve my Emperor,"

Bella raised the gun again at Finn.

Ava smiled. "Are you loyal to the Emperor?"

"I wouldn't have sent my daughter to die if not!"

Ava watched him for a few moments, he wasn't lying. He had actually sent his daughter to die, Ava knew that the Naval Headquarters was destroyed by something looking like a bomb, but... she almost couldn't believe a House Ruler was that reckless.

Unless he was very unhinged and dangerous to let his daughter walk around with an explosive.

Ava took a few steps back.

She wasn't liking this plan now. She couldn't have this man King if he was as dangerous and unhinged as she feared, but at this point she didn't really have much of an option.

Ava was going to have to use him as a source of information at the very least until he either proved too much of a risk to the Empire, she found someone else better suited to the role, or she discovered he was actually a great guy.

She hated how all the sexy men in the Empire were either corrupt, traitorous or just difficult.

"Master," Ronnie said, "we have a problem,"

Ava rolled her eyes and went closer to Ronnie who was intensely studying his built-in holographic computer.

"What?" Ava asked.

"There's a new King and all the Noble Houses have sworn them in. There is nothing we can do," Ronnie said.

Ava smiled. Sometimes her teammates were too dim witted to the true scale of what was really going on, Ava had understood from King Pastor's words that it would be a lot more difficult to complete a Kingmaker operation than she realised at first. But Ava knew there would already be more people ready to take the throne, Ava just needed to turn the tables.

Ava just looked at that beautiful sexy man and she had to admit Finn was amazingly hot. But she doubted he had the skills needed to become king through... more criminal means.

Just by looking at him Ava could tell he might have experienced hardship, but he had always believed in the power of the Process, law and everything that was right about the galaxy. He had no idea about the grey areas that had to be worked in to keep the Empire functioning on even the most basic of levels.

"You are loyal?" Ava asked.

Ava watched Finn intensely as he blinked at her like that wasn't even a real question. She suddenly felt like she was so stupid, childish and like she had no idea about the Empire. Clearly Finn had never questioned his loyalty to the Emperor, so maybe he was an ally after all.

Finn stood up and walked straight up to Ava.

"I would die for the Emperor,"

"You might get your wish," Bella said.

To Ava's surprise, Finn didn't even flinch. He actually seemed happy at that option.

"How do we reclaim my planet in His Name?" Finn asked with a smile.

Ava wondered for a moment if it was a mocking, traitorous or even questioning smile.

But it wasn't.

Ava was looking at the stunning smile of a man who actually believed wholeheartedly in the Empire, what it stood for and he so badly wanted to protect it.

The only problem was, Ava didn't know.

She had no clue how to complete her Kingmaker operation.

Not a single clue.

CHAPTER 8

Finn was shocked at how strange this woman was, she was hot as hell but she was so strange.

Before this whole episode Finn had only heard of the legendary assassins of the Emperor, and now he actually got to stand in front of one of them. That was damn right scary and he didn't know why but he was so drawn to her.

And her name. Ava was a really sexy name that really matched the utterly stunning woman he was standing in front of. Finn was so tempted to run his fingers through her amazingly lifeful brown hair but he knew better than that.

She would probably kill him.

The little apartment they all stood in was awful with its grey concrete walls and utterly foul smell. Finn didn't want to be here, but he just had to be close to this sexy woman.

Granted, Finn seriously would have preferred it if Ava's crazy sidekicks weren't around. The woman with the grenades attached to her waist just looked crazy, and the man with the strange holographic computer in his arm just seemed… out of place.

Finn didn't want to have to deal with these people for any longer than he had to, but he did want to protect the Decimus System and sector and firmly keep it out of the hands of the traitors.

That was the priority.

"Who's the new king?" Finn asked.

The man looked at Ava, she nodded.

"The King is the House Ruler of the House of Darkness," the man said.

Finn swore under his breath. He knew that particular House Ruler very well, Jayden Crow was definitely not a nice man. He was a cold calculating serial killer and Finn hated to imagine how many victims he had killed to get into Pastor's inner circle.

Too many.

"I presume you know of him?" Finn asked.

Ava nodded.

"You might not know," Finn said, choosing his next words carefully, "that he will gladly hand this sector of space over to the Traitors. There are already operatives on the planet,"

Ava smiled. Finn didn't know why, but her smile seemed almost impressed.

"We have the same intelligence. There are five Hydra Legion Operatives on the planet," Ava said.

Finn was still shocked to hear that those evil infiltration specialists were here. it was everyone's worst nightmare.

"We need to kill the House Rulers," Ava said.

Both of Ava's sidekicks smiled in delight. Finn just found that disturbing.

Finn frowned. He wasn't sure if that was the best idea, some of those people were good friends of him for years, it was only over the past year that they had turned against him.

"Is there another way? Maybe we can prosecute-"

Both Ava's sidekicks bursted out laughing.

Ava just looked at Finn. "We are assassins. You cannot prosecute all Traitors, and we need results now. We cannot wait for these House Rulers to hand over the system before we act,"

Finn was surprised at her words. He couldn't understand how someone could sound so cold and uncaring about killing people.

"My people!" Finn shouted. "Everyone in the Western Capital is being transported to the Mind Camps,"

Ava took a few steps closer. "I promise you this. The only way we can stop your people from being transported is to stop this system from Seceding. We need you on the throne,"

Just because she was right. It didn't make it any easier to hear, Finn wanted to be on the throne so badly, but he didn't want his path to it to be so bloody.

"What do you propose?" Finn asked.

Ava looked at the man with the holographic

computer.

"This is Ronnie," she said, "I'm sure he has an idea,"

"Yes Master," Ronnie said.

Then he bought up plans to the main palace. Finn had never seen the massive cathedral-like building in such definition and detail before.

"We need to breach it," Ronnie said. "Once inside we can sneak into the throne room. Kill the King. Then escape,"

Finn just shook his head. "Sounds a little long winded. We cannot keep running into the Palace as each new King is announced,"

Ava cocked her head.

"And you forget," Finn said, "I still need to be made King. That won't happen unless I'm put back into the planet's politics,"

Ava smiled and stood really close to Finn. Finn loved the amazing feeling of her body warmth against his.

"Impossible. I have calculated the odds. It has a certainty of your death. That is not acceptable. The planet deems you a traitor," Ronnie said.

Finn wasn't sure if Ronnie was trying to be touching or not.

Finn stared into Ava's amazing eyes.

"What if I *betray* you? Sound I know where you're hiding. You get captured. I prove my loyalty to the King," Finn said.

Finn's heart pounded in his chest. He didn't

know if this sexy assassin was going to kill him now for even suggesting it. He had just gotten so caught up in the moment.

Ava came so close to his ear that Finn could feel her breath on his face. He loved it.

"I better make it look real," Ava said.

Finn's eyebrows rose.

Ava whacked him round the face.

Finn fell to the ground.

Ava kicked him.

Again and again.

Ava stopped. And to Finn's utter surprise she actually looked a bit upset about it, like she had done the most unthinkable thing possible.

Finn hissed as crippling pain filled his stomach and face. Ava had a hell of a kick and a punch, no wonder she was an assassin.

The woman with the sex grenades came over to Finn and held a gun to his head.

"You go to your people. Reveal our location. Ava gets capture," the woman said.

Finn nodded. This female sidekick seriously scared him, he had no doubt she would kill him if Ava gave the order.

Finn pushed himself up and started to head towards the door.

Fear gripped him. Finn had never done espionage before. He felt like he was way out of his depth.

And Finn knew he could easily hang himself this

time.

But Finn knew there was no coming back now.
It was succeed or fail.
And failure meant death.

CHAPTER 9

Ava was still utterly amazed at how predictably stupid humans were, it didn't matter how many thousands of years passed. Humans were still as stupid today in the age of galactic Empires as they were when humanity crawled out of the oceans back on Ancient Earth.

It was all far too easy to be honest, all Ava had to do was sit there. She loved sitting there in the abandoned apartment pretending to plot some evil scheme when the military had stormed in and three Hydra Operatives were there.

That had been the only surprising thing about it.

Then as Ava planned, the Hydra Operatives would apparently kill her and she was taken right into the deepest darkest depths of the Palace into a little cell.

Ava had actually been expecting something grand considering the Decimus System was one of the richest in the entire Empire. But no, Ava just sat on the cold metal floor in a stinky dirty stone cell with some wonderfully cold iron bars, and a holographic projector playing something in the middle for her.

It had taken Ava a while to figure out what it was, but it was just some propaganda crap the new King was playing. Ava had seen it a thousand times throughout her decades of service, it was the same deep-fake rubbish that pretended the Emperor was evil.

"Hail the Hydra!" a booming voice shouted as it echoed around the cells and stone corridors.

Ava just focused ahead as she saw someone coming out of the darkness.

The air turned slightly in temperature. It was warmer now by a degree and the air smelt slightly of burnt ozone, meaning the person had a personal shield generator in their armour.

A Hydra Operative was coming, that was a certainty.

"Death to the Heads," Ava said calmly.

"You know assassin," the booming voice said, "the Emperor chose us to be his Hydras of war. For each one of us the enemy cut down, two more would spring from the corpse,"

Ava just smiled. She loved listening to the delusions of enemies.

After a few moments a very tall superhuman man stepped out of the darkness. Ava studied him intensely for any weaknesses on his superhuman battle plate that covered every millimetre of his body in thick armour.

There were no weaknesses. No damage. No nothing.

"What was the plan Assassin with the politician?" the Hydra Operative asked.

Ava didn't react.

"The Hydra knows he didn't betray you. These humans might believe his lies, but we do not,"

Ava still didn't react.

"Fine," the Operative said, "but know our ships are coming. This entire planet will become a mind camp for the sector and you will be first in line for… re-education,"

Ava wanted to scream, panic and lash out. But that's what the Hydra idiot wanted, he needed a reaction but Ava had to be smart about this.

Ava knew the idiot was probably aware that her body was a living weapon so he was going to be weary of her. She still needed to kill him though.

"You won't talk to me will you?" the Operative asked.

Ava stood up perfectly straight and walked straight over to the bars.

The Operative pressed himself as the bars too.

"How is Ronnie and Bella these days?" he asked.

Ava forced herself not to react. How the hell did the Hydra know about them? They were meant to be top-secret and… what if they knew who she was?

"Ava Oakley," the Operative said. "Former Soldier in the Empire Army and Interrogator

Specialist for the Emperor's Inquisitors,"

Ava caught a lump in her throat. It was impossible for him to know this, not even her Grand Master knew about this. She had been an Assassin for so long and worked as one during her military service and working her Interrogator service for an Inquisitor.

It was impossible for the traitors to know this.

Not even her team knew this too, and after all the mind-altering surgeries Ava had gone under to mix up her memories in case she was ever sent to the Mind Camps. Ava didn't remember much of what she did during these different periods of her life.

"That's right Ava Oakley," the Operative said. "I know exactly who you are. And no, you will not escape this cell. Just try. Try and kill me I dare you,"

Ava looked up at the prison bars and at the very, very top of the prison cell there was a very slight reflection.

If she wasn't an assassin, Ava would have no clue what it was, but she had used the same technology so many times. If she made an aggressive move, the liquid poison would activate and drip down onto her, paralysing her.

Ava was trapped here.

There would be no escape for her yet.

Ava didn't know how she would.

But she would escape in time.

She just didn't know if there would be a planet, system and sector left to save. When she did.

CHAPTER 10

Finn felt utterly terrible for endangering that beautiful sexy Ava. He felt silly for being so concerned about an assassin, a person who could and would easily kill anyone, but he still felt so terrible about it.

Finn didn't know if he should try to get her out, help her or just let Ava do her own thing. He had never done this before, and he honestly felt so out of his depth. He just hoped that something would go his way.

As Finn stood in a massive cathedral-like throne room with massive floor-to-ceiling stained glass windows showing massive noble battles of the distant past lining every single metre of the throne room. Finn was starting to realise he was a mere mortal compared to these Kings.

He couldn't do anything to stop them.

Then Finn realised that that's what the enemy wanted him to believe. He was a noble protector and servant of the Emperor, he could and would do anything he could to protect his people, his system and most importantly his Emperor.

Finn wasn't a massive fan of the hints of burning sage, orange oil and petrol that clung to the air like an awful plague. It was definitely not the best smell Finn had ever experienced.

That only reinforced how badly this noble planet had fallen in recent days.

"Finn Scott," an elderly female voice said behind him.

Finn didn't react. He kept focusing on the golden throne ahead of him and the utterly disgusting serial killer sitting on it.

Of all the people to become a House Ruler, Finn hated that Jayden Crown had become one. He didn't deserve that honour and it was certainly unhonourable how he got it, and now that he sat on the throne in fine silk robes, golden battle armour and a personal shield generator that made the light shimmer off him. Finn wanted to kill him.

But that wasn't his mission.

"I am glad the old fool is dead," Finn said walking up to Jayden.

Finn felt someone walking very close behind him. He wouldn't have been surprised if it was the House Ruler of the House of Waterlilies.

"What was the plan?" Jayden asked, his voice twisted, psychopathic and rather scary.

Finn smiled. He had to play along and buy the

assassin as much time as possible, and he really hoped Ronnie and that other scary sidekick was watching him.

"The Empire approached me. Thought I was loyal and well, I saw an opportunity. I help them kill stupid old Pastor and we get someone new in charge," Finn said.

Finn felt an icy cold blade press gently against his back.

Jayden nodded regally. Finn hated everything about him.

"You decided to betray them? Seriously? You wanted to betray the people who could give you my throne?" Jayden asked.

Finn gritted his teeth. "I gave someone the throne,"

Finn took a few steps forward. "I demand a place at your side. Without me none of this would be possible. You would be nothing without me!"

Jayden started laughing. Finn felt the blade move away from his back.

"Maybe I did misjudge you," Jayden said. "Maybe you are as corrupt as the rest of us,"

Finn hated doing all of this. He wasn't corrupt, he wasn't a traitor, he wasn't anything.

Jayden gestured Finn to come closer and stand next to him. Finn did. When Finn was standing firmly next to Jayden, he felt his stomach twist like he had just betrayed every single moral fibre of his being.

"Look," Jayden said. "If you were here you could

rule an entire sector of space. A sector that creates so much military might that we could destroy both the Empire and the Traitors,"

Finn forced himself not to laugh. Pastor had truly been a fool, he didn't know how Jayden had manipulated him, but he had. Pastor was firmly going to give over the sector to the Traitors, but Jayden wanted to be far, far more suicidal.

He wanted his own Empire. That was the definition of suicide.

"A critical question remains," Finn said. "How would we get the Traitors and Empire together and cripple them both?"

Then Finn noticed it was the elderly House Ruler from the House of Waterlilies. She was standing there shrouded in darkness holding a knife and wearing a horrible black dress and black veil.

"That is no question," Jayden said. "That is a certainty. We have Empire forces attacking our outer planets at this very moment. We have the traitors zooming towards us as we speak. They will meet,"

"And shall fight," the woman said.

Finn wanted to vomit. This was such a stupidly awful plan that would result in the destruction of the entire sector, but the war had started now.

And there was only one thing Finn could do. He could only become King and help keep the sector in Empire hands as much as possible.

"But you will not be seeing any of this," Jayden said coldly.

Finn frowned. "Why not? You would be nothing without me,"

Jayden laughed. "I know you would never betray the Empire. I know you would die before you ever let me kill the Empire. I know you want to die for your Empire,"

Jayden and the other House Ruler both smiled at Finn.

"Take him to the cells. We have a very entertaining gift for him," Jayden said.

Finn felt a needle thrusted into his neck.

Finn's world went black.

KINGMAKER

CHAPTER 11

Ava was disgusted at the newly crowned King Jayden as she was handcuffed and forced to kneel down in front of him. Ava seriously didn't like the large throne room with its stupid golden throne that was a mere mockery of the Emperor's own one back on Earth.

Ava hated the awful floor-to-ceiling stain glass windows too. She didn't know what pathetic battles and heroes and former Kings it pretended to show.

She was going to destroy all of it.

Ava felt the cold handcuffs chill her skin, and they slowly vibrated, hummed and popped as they struggled to hold her. Ava was flexing her wrists just to test how strong they actually were.

Then Ava noticed a very handsome man laying cold on the floor. It was clearly Finn and Ava surprised herself that she was really concerned about him.

She was an assassin. A cold calculating killer who

never got attached to anything, but somehow that gorgeous sexy man had made her care about him.

Damn him!

After a few moments Finn started to stir and a tall woman shrouded in shadow grabbed him by the neck and threw him over to Ava.

Finn landed hard against the ground and Ava wanted to hug, kiss or just make sure he was okay. But she wasn't going to look weak in front of these mortal fools.

And Ava would be very surprised if the four remaining Hydra Legion Operatives weren't watching.

Jayden clicked his fingers. Ava looked up at the four corners of the throne room and noticed cameras or holographic recorders had been activated.

Ava didn't know why Jayden wanted to effectively stream this, but whatever it was, she didn't like it.

The only possible benefit here was it gave Ronnie something to hack into, and Ava really, really hoped Bella and him were watching and somehow planning their extraction.

Ava just focused on hopefully killing Jayden and every other House Ruler on the planet.

"Activate!" Jayden shouted.

Ava frowned as a thin purple shield activated and wrapped round the throne and the woman shrouded in shadow.

Then four more people (two men, two women) teleported into the throne room holding guns, swords and chains.

Ava recognised them instantly. They were all the other House Rulers on the planet. This was clever and Jayden was far more clever than she ever gave him credit for.

Jayden wanted to eliminate anyone who could stop him. Some of these House Rulers were pro-Empire, others were pro-Traitors, only Jayden was Pro-Independent Empire ruled by him.

Ava couldn't allow any of it.

The two men flew at Ava.

They swung their swords.

They weren't trained. They were foolish.

Ava ducked.

Jumping up.

Into the air.

Kicking out her legs.

She kicked them in the head.

Shattering both of them.

They died instantly.

The two women charged at Finn.

Swinging their chains.

He jumped up.

He couldn't fight.

A woman sliced his chest.

Ava flew forward.

Grabbing their chains.

Ripping it from them.

Ava used the chains as whips.

The chains smashed into one woman.

She screamed in agony.

Her bones smashed. Crunched. Shattered.

She died.

The other woman whipped out a gun.

She aimed.

She fired.

Ava ducked.

Missing the shot.

The woman screamed.

Ava charged.

Finn appeared behind the woman.

Strangulating her.

The woman choked.

Ava went over. Snapped her neck.

After a few moments Ava heard the utterly disgusting sound of Jayden clapping like they had actually achieved something. But they haven't. By killing those men in self-defence they had only reinforced Jayden's position as the new king.

But there was now no one else to take the position as King.

Except Finn.

"Kill them," Jayden said coldly.

Ava didn't know what he was going on about, then Ava felt something vibrate the ground.

The throne room doors slowly opened, Ava felt her stomach churn as she saw a massive bear three times the size of a superhuman warrior of the Emperor and she could see its poisonous teeth drip blood.

Ava picked up a pistol and sword.
Finn picked up another sword.
Ava just looked at him.
This was going to be a hell of a fight.

CHAPTER 12

Finn was utterly shocked as he stared at the disgusting massive bear that seriously terrified him. He wasn't a fighter. A killer. He was just a politician, one that was clearly going to die at any second.

Finn needed an escape plan but he couldn't see any. All he could see was the massive ugly bear, those pathetic floor-to-ceiling stained glass windows and that idiot Jayden.

But Finn had to protect his beautiful Ava no matter what, and he was going to sacrifice himself for her regardless of her mission.

The bear charged.

Its paws pounding the floor.

Finn jumped out the way.

Ava emptied her gun into the creature.

Its fur burned away.

The creature didn't stop.

The creature swung around.

It charged at Ava.

Finn charged over.

Finn swung his sword.

The creature kicked him.

Sending him flying across the room.

Finn smashed into a large red window.

It cracked.

Finn didn't care.

The Creature had Ava pinned.

Its jaws were getting closer.

Finn rushed over.

He jumped into the air.

He thrusted his sword into the creature.

Behind the shoulder blade.

The creature roared.

It whacked Finn with his paws.

Finn flew across the room.

Whacking into the large red window again.

It cracked even more.

Ava threw the gun into the creature's mouth.

The creature was struggling to move.

It was slower.

Finn smashed his feet on the ground.

The Creature stared at him. It charged. Finn braced himself.

The Creature kept charging it was going so fast.

The Creature was so close.

Finn jumped out the way.

The Creature smashed into the large red window.

Shattering it.

The Creature kept moving.

Flying through the window.

The Creature slashed Finn's leg.

Its claws grabbed on.

The Creature was falling out.

Finn grabbed onto the edge of the window.

Ava grabbed his hands.

The Creature ripped out chunks of his flesh.

The Creature fell hundreds of metres before its smashed onto the marble floor outside. Ava helped Finn back into the throne room, and Finn forced himself not to cry at the extreme crippling pain that flooded through his body.

Blood was pouring out of the wound on his leg and Finn was certain he was going to die. But he made sure he stared at Ava's stunning face one last time.

He wanted to kiss Ava's soft sexy lips so much, but they were just out of reach.

"Make you a deal Ava," Jayden said.

Ava wrapped her hands firmly round Finn's wound and elevated his wound far above his heart. The bleeding thankfully slowed. Maybe she really did care about him.

"If you kill Finn for me," Jayden said, "I will give you full immunity in my Empire and you can come and go as you please. You can kill whatever of my criminals you want, just kill Finn Scott for me,"

Ava laughed. Finn was surprised at the laugh. It wasn't sexy, attractive or anything like it. It was scary, it was the laugh of a cold calculating psychopath that was ready to kill everyone and everything she could.

"This is not your Empire!" Ava shouted. "This belongs to Him On Earth and the Emperor will not keep you pathetic weak traitors alive!"

The entire palace and throne room vibrated. Finn wanted to get out. He didn't know what was going on.

"This planet, this system, this sector belongs to the Emperor. And you will not keep it so easily!" Ava shouted.

Jayden just smiled. "And tell me assassin, what can you do about it. Your operation is a failure. Finn will die. There is no one left to become King for your corrupt Emperor,"

Finn just watched Ava laugh at Jayden. She didn't seem concerned in the slightest.

Ava just pointed her sword at Jayden, and Finn couldn't deny she was sexy in that pose.

"True, true, true," Ava said. "You might have killed Finn. But there are three people you never thought to get rid of,"

Jayden's smile deepened. "And who are they?"

Ava gave Finn a psychopathic smile. "Me and my friends. Do it!"

The entire palace shook.

The stained glass windows shattered.

Bella stormed into the throne room.

Sword and gun raised.

Ronnie stumbled in behind her. A cannon built into his arm.

The thin shield around Jayden deactivated.
Finn smiled. Jayden was going to die.

CHAPTER 13

Ava flat out loved her amazing team as they stormed in behind her. She knew she could trust them to help. She damn well loved them!

Ava listened to the air hum, crackled and pop as the shield deactivated in front of Jayden and she charged.

Jayden whipped out a sword.

Ava loved it when they fought.

It was so useless.

Ava flew at Jayden.

She jumped into the air.

Kicking him in the head.

He stumbled back.

Bella shot him in the knee.

He hissed.

He screamed.

Ava slashed his throat.

Jayden's blood sprayed up the walls, throne and floor.

Jayden tried to grab his throat.

Ava sliced off his hands and heads and legs just to make sure he was completely dead.

Ava was about to spin round to kill the woman shrouded in shadows but she was gone. There wasn't even a trace of her ever being there.

But at least King Jayden Crow, traitor to the Empire and more ironically a traitor to the traitors, was dead. And now the Decimus system and the larger sector could safely be returned to Empire hands.

Ava spun around.

Ava rushed over to Finn. She couldn't let him die. He was so important to the mission, if Finn died then the sector might never return to Empire hands, and the Empire would be damned.

But as much as Ava hated it, she knew Finn was more important than just the mission. She cared about him, she hated to feel so drawn to this sexy handsome man, but she really was.

"Master," Ronnie said as Ava just stared into Finn's eyes as they were slowly going more and more distant.

"Yes," Ava said, trying to keep her voice level.

"Enemy troopers incoming. Orders are shoot to kill. We have to go," Ronnie said.

"I can't... I can't leave him," Ava said, as she watched more and more and more of Finn's blood pool on the ground.

Ronnie shook his head and whacked his cannon

against the floor. it immediately started humming, splattering and sounding like it might explode.

Ronnie started hissing and Ava frowned as she saw in agony. She didn't like seeing her friends like this. Then his built-in cannon glowed bright red.

Ava jumped out the way.

Ronnie smashed the red hot cannon onto Finn's leg and thankfully enough the bleeding stopped.

Then Ronnie ripped off the cannon for his arm, so now he only had one arm.

"Where's your normal one?" Ava asked.

Ronnie just looked at her. "Left it at base. Didn't think I needed to bring a spare,"

"Thank you," Ava said kindly.

Ronnie just nodded.

Bullets screamed into the throne. Ten golden armoured soldiers stormed into the room.

Ava laughed. She picked up two swords.

She charged.

Bullets screamed past her.

The guards were scared.

They were panicking.

Ava slid across the floor.

Knocking the legs out from under three men.

Bella shot them in the head.

Ava leapt up.

Swinging her swords.

Slashing their throats.

Blood rained down on the throne room.

One man jumped on Ava.

Ava jumped back onto the floor.

The man's spine cracked.

Ava jumped up.

Ramming her swords into his eyes.

With all the royal guards (for now at least) dead, Ava was relieved to see Ronnie helping Finn stand upright. He was alive and Ava would never admit it, but that made her so happy.

She actually felt like a little schoolgirl again back at the assassin training camps when she met her first love. A really cute boy that was killed on a training mission by the foul traitors.

Ava loved how Finn made her feel… like a real person again after decades of cold killing in the Assassin Guilds. She wanted so badly to kiss him, love him and just… do all the adult things she had never done to anyone but a target.

And Finn was not a target to kill. He was a target to love, protect and maybe even treasure.

"Master," Ronnie said, "Five traitor fleets have entered the system,"

Ava's eyes widened. There were at least five ships in each fleet and five thousand soldiers on each ship. That was a hell of a lot of firepower.

"Our mission isn't done anyway," Ava said.

"What do you mean?" Finn asked weakly. "I thought I was now King,"

Ava smiled. She was fairly sure one couldn't simply declare themselves king without making a formal speech or something, but that was too dangerous at the moment.

"There are still four Hydra Legion Operatives. They probably started all of this in the first place, then Jayden took over their plan. Those Operatives are why those Fleets are here, and now their focus will shift," Ava said.

Bella nodded. "Strategy dictates their focus will change from Changing Governments to Destruction. The Operatives will want to destroy anything that could be used to stop the traitor fleets from coming in,"

"But the Fleets aren't Hydra, Master," Ronnie said.

Ava shrugged. Out of the six traitor legions of superhuman warriors, whilst it was true Hydra operatives and soldiers tended to only work with their own, it wasn't exactly unheard of for them to work with the other traitor legions.

At the end of the day, they were all trying to claim the Empire for their united Leader the warrior known as the Lord of War.

"Raven Crow Legion are incoming along with a brand new fleet that is right behind them, Master,"

"Who's the new Legion?" Ava asked.

"World Burners," Ronnie said.

"Shit!" Ava said.

Ava just paced around for a few moments. Then she realised that the Hydra Legion weren't just infiltration specialists that was a relatively new skill, they were mainly superhuman spies.

It was the Raven Crow that could infiltrate everywhere and sabotage entire solar systems without anyone ever knowing they had been there. Or when people did realise the Raven Crow was involved, they had already been got for weeks or months or even years.

But the World Burners were what was concerning Ava. Their real name was Galaxy Burners, because all they wanted to do was burn the entire Empire and galaxy in the name of the Lord of War, they were some of the most brutal superhumans Ava had ever fought against.

She couldn't allow the World Burners to land planetside under any circumstances.

Ava looked at Finn. "I need to know where is your Orbital Defence Fortress,"

Ava watched the sweat start to drip down Finn's face. She didn't know how he managed to make that look attractive but he did somehow, but she knew his body needed to be treated.

Thankfully she had access to advance medical supplies through her assassin contacts to help him. She was pleased that she had bought some supplies against the protests of her Grand Master back in the Emperor's Shadow.

"We don't have one," Finn said.

"How!" Ava shouted. "You're a critical planet that controls an entire sector of space. How the hell do you not have a orbital defence cannon that could smash anything in orbit into chunks of nothing!"

Finn tapped on the ground before in collapsed into Ronnie's (real) arm.

Ava waved Ronnie away. "Get him the drugs from the Emperor's Shadow. I need him,"

Bella just smiled. Ava pretended to look mad at her.

Ava looked at the floor and realised something she had completely dismissed before.

When she was looking at the detailed plans of the Palace, she had completely dismissed the massive empty space below the palace. She had wondered if there was a nuclear bunker or something similar under the palace.

What if there was something else?

Something more offensive.

Something that could be a very tempting target for superhuman spies.

Ava had to go under the palace.

CHAPTER 14

Finn was really surprised at the amazing medical supplies, drugs and other weird and wonderful supplies the assassins of the Emperor had access to. Finn was now basically healed and he felt amazing.

Finn was still getting used to his cybernetic leg but at least he could walk and he felt powerful.

But now he absolutely had to stop these superhumans from sabotaging the only weapon that could defend his planet from the incoming traitor fleet.

As Finn walked closely behind Ava, Bella and Ronnie (who had a machine gun for an arm now) through a long metal tunnel, he was starting to realise how serious the threat was.

He was about to fight superhuman warriors. He had never ever even thought about this before, but at least Ava had given him an adapted gun that fired the same explosive rounds as the superhumans. He really wondered what else the assassins had on the

Emperor's shadow.

Ava raised her fist and everyone stopped.

"Hail The Hydra," a booming voice said from up ahead.

Finn raised his gun. Everyone else did too, but Ava seemed to recognise the man. All Finn saw was an ugly man cladded completely in thick metal armour. He had no clue how she would recognise someone.

"You cannot win," Ava said.

Finn looked around for some cover in case a fight broke out. There was none. They would be completely exposed if the enemy started shooting.

Bella unclipped a grenade from her waist.

"Ava Oakley. You cannot stop us. I have killed assassins before for the Hydra and your fate will be no different," the booming man said.

Ava clicked her fingers. "We shall see,"

Bella threw the grenade.

Smoke filled the tunnel.

Finn saw the others charge forward.

Finn flew at the enemy.

He couldn't see them.

Bullets fired.

The enemy laughed.

They attacked.

He couldn't see anyone.

Something massive grabbed Finn.

Tackling him to the ground.

A massive hand gripped his jaw.

Pain flooded him.

Finn raised his gun.

He fired.

The enemy hissed.

Finn pushed the superhuman off him.

The enemy kicked him.

Finn fired again.

The enemy hissed.

Finn couldn't see him.

Someone got him in a headlock from behind.

Finn was being dragged away from the fighting.

Out of the smoke.

Finn wanted to be grateful but then he realised he was shrouded in shadow and he just knew he was being held in a headlock by that awful House Ruler of the House of Waterlilies. He hated her.

She pushed him away.

Finn turned and just looked at her.

She was disgusting.

The woman whipped out a longsword.

Finn shot her.

The bullet smashed into her.

But no damage was done and the woman simply stood there like nothing had ever happened to her.

The woman flew at him.

She swung her sword.

Finn ducked.

She kept swinging.

Finn ducked.

He rolled on the floor.

He jumped up.

The sword rushed past him.

Finn ran.

The woman kicked him into the floor.

Climbing on top of him.

Pressing the sword against his throat.

Finn just reacted.

He pointed the gun behind him.

The sword pressed deeper.

Finn fired.

The sword fell onto the ground and a very heavy woman fell onto him as her brain matter, blood and charred skull fragment spattered onto his back.

The House Ruler of the House of Waterlilies was dead. The last traitorous member of the Noble Houses was dead.

And Finn had to find his team.

They had to kill the traitors.

They had to save his planet.

Then Finn had to ask Ava on a date.

CHAPTER 15

Ava was completely impressed sexy handsome Finn killed that murderous traitor woman. That was impressive. Now she had to do her part as the group entered a massive spherical room with an immense ringed-platform around the outside.

"Enemy contacts," Ronnie said.

Ava nodded but she knew the enemy wouldn't attack them just yet. From decades of killing she just knew that the enemy wanted her to look at what they had achieved.

It was the fatal flaw of the traitor legions.

Ava just stared at the very centre of the spherical room where an immense ball of energy hummed, buzzed and crackled.

Now Ava understood what Finn meant when he said that the system didn't have an orbital defence cannon or something like that.

Instead this system had a much rarer and more dangerous type of defence. If this immense ball of energy was launched, then it would easily fly into orbit, explode and annihilate any ships within the system.

But Ava doubted the traitors knew about the other side effects. It would completely scour this planet into a lifeless rock and it would collapse any society within the system.

This would annihilate the traitor and Empire forces alike.

Ava heard the heavy armoured boots of four remaining Hydra Operatives stomp towards them.

"Beautiful isn't it Ava?" the man with the booming voice asked.

Ava nodded. There was so much death, destruction and chaos. Billions would die with a simple launch.

She couldn't allow that.

Ava pointed her gun at the heavily armoured Operatives.

"Ronnie," Ava said coldly.

"Yes Master,"

"Hack into the computer system and make sure the roof can never be opened," Ava said.

Ronnie nodded and tapped the machine gun mounted to his arm and a little holographic computer popped out. His cybernetic arms were amazing.

She could have sworn she heard the Operatives gasp inside their helmets.

The Operatives pointed their guns at Ronnie. He didn't even flinch.

"Return to your Fleet and leave," Ava said.

The booming man laughed. His laugh sounded so horrible, twisted and disease-ridden.

"Or what Ava? You wouldn't kill yourself in the process. You have too many enemies to kill for your corrupt Emperor," he said.

Finn pointed his gun at the immense energy ball.

Ava did the same. She didn't know if this was wise or stupid. They could kill themselves if this plan failed.

"If we fire. The energy ball will become unstable and without the roof being opened. The energy ball will explode and be contained in this chamber,"

The Operatives looked at each other.

They walked towards Ava. She didn't flinch. She had to remain strong.

"Master," Ronnie said, "I am unable to complete objective. Hydra has infected the system and…"

Ronnie's computer arm whipped out a gun. His computer arm pointed it at Ava.

"Master? They've hacked me arm!"

Ava laughed. That was clever. But the traitors had just tried to kill her friend.

This wasn't fun anymore. Ava didn't know how but she was going to kill these superhuman traitors and protect everyone.

Ava looked at the holographic bracelet on her wrist and she pressed a little button. She really hoped her emergency teleporter would work again.

"Open it!" Ava shouted.

Everyone went silent.

The Operatives nodded at Ronnie.

Ava just looked at Finn. He wasn't scared. He was actually excited.

Ronnie's computer arm relaxed itself and he openly typed away at it.

A few moments later the entire chamber shook as presumably the palace above them was being annihilated to give the energy ball a clear shot.

Ava wanted to shake her head or something. This energy ball was meant to be used as an ultimate failsafe, not a means of killing some Operatives and perhaps themselves.

Ava just hoped the teleporter would work.

The man with the booming voice put his gun straight to Ava's head.

"I'll give you one chance to leave Ava Oakley," he said.

Ava just shook her head. "Now!"

Ava ducked.

The booming man fired.

Ava emptied her gun into the energy ball.

Finn did the same.

Bella flew at the traitors.

The energy ball shrieked.

It crackled.

Lightning bolts shot out.

Ronnie closed the roof.

The energy ball turned unstable.

"You're gonna kill us!" an Operative shouted.

Ava flew at her team.
Grabbing them.
They all grabbed onto her.
"No. Only you!" Ava shouted.
They didn't teleport away.
Lightning bolts shot out.
It zapped the traitors.
Their flesh cooked.
They screamed.
Smoke poured from their armour.
Fear gripped Ava.
She looked at Finn.
She couldn't have him die.
Ava didn't want to lose him.
She loved him!
Ronnie pushed himself away.
He started swiping at his holographic computer.
Lightning bolts shot out around him.
The roof opened.
Ronnie smiled.
A lightning bolt cooked him.
He died smiling.
They still weren't teleporting.
The chamber started to collapse.
Bella screamed.
The energy ball expanded.
Sweat poured down Ava.
Ava just stared into Finn's amazing blue stunning eyes.
Finn leant closer.

Lighting shot towards them.
Blue smoke wrapped round them.
They teleported away.

CHAPTER 16

Finn was completely amazed at how the past week had flown by with all the annihilation of the traitor fleets by the Empire forces, the resupplying of the entire system and making sure that no more traitor elements were alive in the entire sector.

Before all this chaos Finn might have been surprised it had taken the Empire only a week to purge the entire sector of the traitors, but he had no doubt that beautiful Ava was not the only Agent of the Emperor that had been sent to deal with the threat.

And maybe that was Finn's favourite part of the entire week. He had been spending so much time with Ava and he damn well loved it. He got to learn that she was actually a lot of fun, very flexible and really knew tons of different things about the Empire, from music to history to the sciences. She was an expert in them all.

Finn stared out over the massive glass windows

of an Emperor-class destroyer with the massive oval bridge with all its holographic computers behind him. Finn just listened to all the reports coming in behind him from forces all over the sector.

Finn heard everyone muttering, relaying orders and just working as hard as they could to protect the Empire they loved.

Even the air smelt of their hard work with hints of sweat, burnt coffee and energy drinks filling the air that left a very strange calming yet strange taste on his tongue of coffee cake.

Finn really did love seeing everyone working away up here, it actually reminded him of his daughter a little. She had worked so hard to protect him, the planet and the Empire that she had actually died in the process.

Without her Finn knew what would have happened and he didn't like it. Ava's ship would have been destroyed, the traitors would have been able to mount a great defence against the Empire forces and the entire sector would have fallen into traitor hands.

Finn would have never allowed that. The Decimus system produced way too much firepower for that to happen.

But apparently Ava knew all these things because she needed to become an expert in different topics to seduce different targets, but he didn't care. Finn just loved her, Ava was so smart beautiful and just amazing that he never wanted her to leave him.

Finn just kept staring down at his amazing planet

below, he had just returned from there after giving a massive speech, ceremony and thank yous to all the survivors and thankfully there were some civilians that tried (and failed) to mount resistance against the Hydra forces.

So Finn had thanked them like any King should. Their resistance didn't actually achieve or do anything, but that wasn't the point.

The point was his amazing people had tried to protect the Empire he loved, and at the end of the day that's all that mattered. Because in the bitter end if the traitors had won, then that type of resistance would have been their only hope.

"King Finn Scott," a man said behind him.

Finn turned around and he instantly fell to his knees. The man behind him was made up of a golden hologram and he was best looking man Finn had ever seen.

This man had a stunning face, stunning eyes and the most ornate armour he had ever seen.

It had to be the Emperor.

Finn instantly felt like such a fool, and like he was in the presence of a god.

"Rise," the Emperor said, gently.

Finn couldn't help but obey. The Emperor's voice sounded so commanding, booming yet there was such a warmth to it too.

"My Lord Emperor," Finn said bowing his head.

The Emperor gestured to the planet down below.

"Congratulations on your appointment," he said.

"It was always going to be you my friend. Can I rely on you to guide your system?"

Finn wanted to pull a strange face like that was the most stupidest question someone had ever asked him, but he was hardly going to do that to the Emperor.

"Of course my Lord. It will be my honour and I will transform this system and sector so we can be even more helpful to the Empire,"

The Emperor smiled. Finn just stared for a moment, he wanted to see any signs of malice, hate or even just plain out manipulation. But the Emperor wasn't like that, he really cared about Finn, his subjects and the entire Empire.

He loved humankind, just like Finn.

"Then King Scott," the Emperor said, "I wish you the best of luck and if you ever need anything, you only need to call,"

Finn instantly raised his hand and touched the hologram. Finn's heart pounded. He thought he was going to die.

But the Emperor only smiled. "I am very well informed King Scott. You have my blessing to ask Ava Oakley out, but only if she wills it,"

Finn's mouth just dropped. It was impossible for the Emperor (who was back on Earth) to know of what he wanted, he hadn't told anyone in the past week about his feelings.

The Emperor just kindly laughed and disappeared.

"A God Amongst Men indeed," Finn muttered to himself.

So with everything done, with him being King and him having the blessing of the Emperor himself about Ava, he just had to ask her the most important question he had ever asked.

But whatever the answer, Finn still knew it would be amazing. His body felt wonderful just thinking about her, and he really, really did love her.

Especially after she had saved him, his planet and most importantly his future.

CHAPTER 17

Ava completely loved watching all the amazing reports of the death, destruction and killing that poured into the Emperor-class Destroyer as Ava stood in front of a large holographic table that showed massive chunks of annihilated warships just floating there, just traitorous crew being sucked into the cold dark void of space.

The large oval bridge was always a hive of activity during these sorts of clear up operations, there was always so much killing, destroying and sabotaging to do.

And Ava loved it.

Over the past week when she hadn't been protecting Finn from assassination plots, poisonings and everything else that Finn didn't realise was going on, Ava had jumped on a few missions to the other planets in the solar system killing the traitors.

But she couldn't admit this in front of anyone, she had really missed Finn when he wasn't with her.

It was a completely strange, alien and outrageous way for an assassin to feel, but she did.

Ava honestly felt so lost without him, and even now as she watched him stare out over his planet and talk to the Emperor himself (which was great considering Finn and her were the only people concentrating enough to see him), Ava just wanted to go over to him and kiss and hug him.

Bella slowly walked over to the holographic table and stood opposite Ava. And as much as Ava wanted to smile and be happy to see her Junior Assassin, she still wanted to see her other "little sidekick" as Finn called him.

Ronnie had always been such an amazing, positive and helpful friend. He was probably the only cool one of the group with his interchangeable arms that were so helpful.

And Ava felt like she was throwing everything away by wanting to be with Finn. Would Ronnie want that?

After all he did sacrifice himself so Ava could go on other missions and protect the Empire. So wasn't it her duty to him, the Emperor and the entire Empire to keep serving and just abandon this entire sector of space?

Ava just shook her head. She honestly didn't know, after a lifetime (to most normal humans) of hunting down the enemies of man, killing and sabotaging them. Ava just didn't know how to be normal anymore.

Even if she did leave all this behind, could she really be happy living as a Queen or something in government?

Ava just looked at Bella who was smiling at her. Then Ava realised that Bella actually was the daughter of a former-Noble House.

"Say it," Ava said.

"There is more than one way to serve Him on Earth. You don't always need to be travelling, hunting or destroying the enemy with a blade," Bella said.

Ava went over to her. "What do you mean?"

Ava had no clue how she was telling the truth.

"There are thousands of types of Agents of The Emperor, and government officials are one. You could still protect the system from within, you will always be an assassin A… Master,"

Ava just nodded. It made sense in a way, she would always have her training and at least if she was inside the heart of the Decimus system and wider sector, she would eventually become the heart of it. She would be able to hear, detect and deal with any threats before they got too dangerous to the wider Empire.

She could still serve the Empire she loved. And be with Finn.

Yet Ava would be lying if she said she wanted Bella to leave her and go and serve a different Master Assassin. Ava hadn't realised it until now that she actually never wanted her team to leave her, they were her family, her best friends and damn good at their job.

"Don't leave me," Ava said, like a little schoolgirl who was being abandoned by their parents on the first day of school.

Bella smiled. "Come on boss, you know that wasn't going to happen,"

"What wasn't?" Finn asked.

"Master," Bella said, bowing her head as she walked away.

Ava just stared at that sexy handsome man with his amazing body, jawline and those stunning blue eyes that she just had to stare into when she thought she was going to die earlier.

Ava didn't want any messy talk about their feelings to spoil the end of the mission. Just yet. So Ava did the only thing she knew how to do, work.

"I found out who that booming voice man was," Ava said.

Finn folded his arms and smiled. "How? He seemed to know everything about you, your team and my planet,"

"You forget," Ava said, "these are Hydra Legion Operatives. Superhuman spies. They specialise in getting information, and I knew the booming voice man from my past,"

Finn stepped closer and Ava closed the feeling of his warm body radiating onto her skin.

"I was a former Interrogator 'torture specialist you might say' for an Inquisitor and we dealt with a Hydra Legion warband before. Turns out it was the same band as this one,"

Finn just shook his head. "I cannot believe the Inquisitor just released those traitors. I believed the Inquisitor would just kill them,"

Damn. Ava had just walked into a very classic trap and one she didn't exactly know to get out of. The Inquisitor had traded these particular Operatives in exchange for information on the Lord of War's location.

To Ava it always seemed like the Hydra Legion were almost mercenary in their loyalties. But the information was good and Ava had even heard a rumour that the Lord of War had been stabbed.

A very impossible feat.

But Ava couldn't tell Finn how the Empire had done a very dodgy deal with the traitors themselves for the greater good of the Empire. It would break his heart, and Ava wasn't going to do that to the man... to the man she loved so much.

Ava simply wrapped her hands around his. "It's complicated,"

Finn nodded and smiled. "I don't doubt it. And I was wondering if you... you would like to go on a date with me?"

Ava hadn't been expecting that, but given Finn had just spoken to the Emperor. It actually made sense why Finn had had enough courage to ask her out, and whatever happened next Ava just knew it was going to be great, wonderful and amazing.

Not because she was serving anyone, but because

she was with Finn.

Ava didn't really know where the future would take her, but she knew a few things. She would always be an assassin fighting to protect the ones she loved, she would always have a great Junior Assassin around her, and most importantly she would be with the stunning man she loved more than anything.

And that made her the happiest woman alive.

GET YOUR FREE EXCLUSIVE GARRO SHORT STORY HERE!

https://www.subscribepage.com/garrosignup

About the author:

Connor Whiteley is the author of over 60 books in the sci-fi fantasy, nonfiction psychology and books for writer's genre and he is a Human Branding Speaker and Consultant.

He is a passionate warhammer 40,000 reader, psychology student and author.

Who narrates his own audiobooks and he hosts The Psychology World Podcast.

All whilst studying Psychology at the University of Kent, England.

Also, he was a former Explorer Scout where he gave a speech to the Maltese President in August 2018 and he attended Prince Charles' 70th Birthday Party at Buckingham Palace in May 2018.

Plus, he is a self-confessed coffee lover!

OTHER SHORT STORIES BY CONNOR WHITELEY

<u>Mystery Short Stories:</u>
Poison In The Candy Cane
Christmas Innocence
You Better Watch Out
Christmas Theft
Trouble In Christmas
Smell of The Lake
Problem In A Car
Theft, Past and Team
Embezzler In The Room
A Strange Way To Go
A Horrible Way To Go
Ann Awful Way To Go
An Old Way To Go
A Fishy Way To Go
A Pointy Way To Go
A High Way To Go
A Fiery Way To Go
A Glassy Way To Go
A Chocolatey Way To Go
Kendra Detective Mystery Collection Volume 1
Kendra Detective Mystery Collection Volume 2
Stealing A Chance At Freedom

Glassblowing and Death
Theft of Independence
Cookie Thief
Marble Thief
Book Thief
Art Thief
Mated At The Morgue
The Big Five Whoopee Moments
Stealing An Election
Mystery Short Story Collection Volume 1
Mystery Short Story Collection Volume 2

<u>Science Fiction Short Stories:</u>
The First Rememberer
Life of A Rememberer
System of Wonder
Lifesaver
Remarkable Way She Died
The Interrogation of Annabella Stormic
Blade of The Emperor
Arbiter's Truth
Computation of Battle
Old One's Wrath
Puppets and Masters
Ship of Plague
Interrogation
Edge of Failure

One Way Choice
Acceptable Losses
Balance of Power
Good Idea At The Time
Escape Plan
Escape In The Hesitation
Inspiration In Need
Singing Warriors
Knowledge is Power
Killer of Polluters
Climate of Death
The Family Mailing Affair
Defining Criminality
The Martian Affair
A Cheating Affair
The Little Café Affair
Mountain of Death
Prisoner's Fight
Claws of Death
Bitter Air
Honey Hunt
Blade On A Train

<u>Fantasy Short Stories:</u>
City of Snow
City of Light
City of Vengeance
Dragons, Goats and Kingdom
Smog The Pathetic Dragon
Don't Go In The Shed
The Tomato Saver
The Remarkable Way She Died
The Bloodied Rose
Asmodia's Wrath
Heart of A Killer
Emissary of Blood
Dragon Coins
Dragon Tea
Dragon Rider
Sacrifice of the Soul
Heart of The Flesheater
Heart of The Regent
Heart of The Standing
Feline of The Lost
Heart of The Story
City of Fire
Awaiting Death

Other books by Connor Whiteley:

Bettie English Private Eye Series
A Very Private Woman
The Russian Case
A Very Urgent Matter
A Case Most Personal
Trains, Scots and Private Eyes
The Federation Protects

The Fireheart Fantasy Series
Heart of Fire
Heart of Lies
Heart of Prophecy
Heart of Bones
Heart of Fate

City of Assassins (Urban Fantasy)
City of Death
City of Marytrs
City of Pleasure
City of Power

Agents of The Emperor
Return of The Ancient Ones
Vigilance
Angels of Fire
Kingmaker

The Garro Series- Fantasy/Sci-fi
GARRO: GALAXY'S END
GARRO: RISE OF THE ORDER
GARRO: END TIMES
GARRO: SHORT STORIES
GARRO: COLLECTION
GARRO: HERESY
GARRO: FAITHLESS
GARRO: DESTROYER OF WORLDS
GARRO: COLLECTIONS BOOK 4-6
GARRO: MISTRESS OF BLOOD
GARRO: BEACON OF HOPE
GARRO: END OF DAYS

Winter Series- Fantasy Trilogy Books
WINTER'S COMING
WINTER'S HUNT
WINTER'S REVENGE
WINTER'S DISSENSION

Miscellaneous:
RETURN
FREEDOM
SALVATION
Reflection of Mount Flame
The Masked One
The Great Deer

All books in 'An Introductory Series':

BIOLOGICAL PSYCHOLOGY 3RD EDITION

COGNITIVE PSYCHOLOGY THIRD EDITION

SOCIAL PSYCHOLOGY- 3RD EDITION

ABNORMAL PSYCHOLOGY 3RD EDITION

PSYCHOLOGY OF RELATIONSHIPS- 3RD EDITION

DEVELOPMENTAL PSYCHOLOGY 3RD EDITION

HEALTH PSYCHOLOGY

RESEARCH IN PSYCHOLOGY

A GUIDE TO MENTAL HEALTH AND TREATMENT AROUND THE WORLD- A GLOBAL LOOK AT DEPRESSION

FORENSIC PSYCHOLOGY

THE FORENSIC PSYCHOLOGY OF THEFT, BURGLARY AND OTHER CRIMES AGAINST PROPERTY

CRIMINAL PROFILING: A FORENSIC PSYCHOLOGY GUIDE TO FBI PROFILING AND GEOGRAPHICAL AND STATISTICAL PROFILING.

CLINICAL PSYCHOLOGY

FORMULATION IN PSYCHOTHERAPY

KINGMAKER

PERSONALITY PSYCHOLOGY AND INDIVIDUAL DIFFERENCES
CLINICAL PSYCHOLOGY REFLECTIONS VOLUME 1
CLINICAL PSYCHOLOGY REFLECTIONS VOLUME 2
CULT PSYCHOLOGY
Police Psychology

Companion guides:
BIOLOGICAL PSYCHOLOGY 2ND EDITION WORKBOOK
COGNITIVE PSYCHOLOGY 2ND EDITION WORKBOOK
SOCIOCULTURAL PSYCHOLOGY 2ND EDITION WORKBOOK
ABNORMAL PSYCHOLOGY 2ND EDITION WORKBOOK
PSYCHOLOGY OF HUMAN RELATIONSHIPS 2ND EDITION WORKBOOK
HEALTH PSYCHOLOGY WORKBOOK
FORENSIC PSYCHOLOGY WORKBOOK

Audiobooks by Connor Whiteley:
BIOLOGICAL PSYCHOLOGY
COGNITIVE PSYCHOLOGY
SOCIOCULTURAL PSYCHOLOGY
ABNORMAL PSYCHOLOGY
PSYCHOLOGY OF HUMAN RELATIONSHIPS
HEALTH PSYCHOLOGY
DEVELOPMENTAL PSYCHOLOGY
RESEARCH IN PSYCHOLOGY
FORENSIC PSYCHOLOGY
GARRO: GALAXY'S END
GARRO: RISE OF THE ORDER
GARRO: SHORT STORIES
GARRO: END TIMES
GARRO: COLLECTION
GARRO: HERESY
GARRO: FAITHLESS
GARRO: DESTROYER OF WORLDS
GARRO: COLLECTION BOOKS 4-6
GARRO: COLLECTION BOOKS 1-6

Business books:

TIME MANAGEMENT: A GUIDE FOR STUDENTS AND WORKERS

LEADERSHIP: WHAT MAKES A GOOD LEADER? A GUIDE FOR STUDENTS AND WORKERS.

BUSINESS SKILLS: HOW TO SURVIVE THE BUSINESS WORLD? A GUIDE FOR STUDENTS, EMPLOYEES AND EMPLOYERS.

BUSINESS COLLECTION

GET YOUR FREE BOOK AT:
WWW.CONNORWHITELEY.NET

www.ingramcontent.com/pod-product-compliance
Lightning Source LLC
LaVergne TN
LVHW011844060526
838200LV00054B/4157